Marx Machiavelli Chesterton Emerson Joyce
Abbott Hardy Montaigne Cooper Austen
Defoe Melville Haggard Hugo
Christie Eliot Grimm
Stoker Carroll Molière
Wilde Maupassant Byron
Schiller
Garnett Einstein Fitzgerald Engels Smith
Goethe Hawthorne Kafka
Cotton Dostoyevsky Hall
Baum Kipling Doyle Willis
Leslie Dumas Henry Nietzsche
Flaubert Turgenev Balzac
Stockton Vatsyayana Crane
Burroughs Whitman Verne
Curtis Tocqueville Gogol Vinci
Homer Widger Tolstoy Busch
Darwin Thoreau Scott
Potter Freud Zola Plato Twain
Lawrence
Kant Jowett Stevenson Dickens
Andersen Burton Hesse Harte
London Descartes Cervantes
Poe Aristotle Wells Voltaire
Hale James Hastings Cooke
Bunner Shakespeare
Richter Chambers Irving
Doré Swift Dante Chekhov da Shaw Wodehouse Benedict Alcott
Pushkin
Newton

tredition®

tredition was established in 2006 by Sandra Latusseck and Soenke Schulz. Based in Hamburg, Germany, tredition offers publishing solutions to authors and publishing houses, combined with worldwide distribution of printed and digital book content. tredition is uniquely positioned to enable authors and publishing houses to create books on their own terms and without conventional manufacturing risks.

For more information please visit: www.tredition.com

TREDITION CLASSICS

This book is part of the TREDITION CLASSICS series. The creators of this series are united by passion for literature and driven by the intention of making all public domain books available in printed format again - worldwide. Most TREDITION CLASSICS titles have been out of print and off the bookstore shelves for decades. At tredition we believe that a great book never goes out of style and that its value is eternal. Several mostly non-profit literature projects provide content to tredition. To support their good work, tredition donates a portion of the proceeds from each sold copy. As a reader of a TREDITION CLASSICS book, you support our mission to save many of the amazing works of world literature from oblivion. See all available books at www.tredition.com.

Project Gutenberg

The content for this book has been graciously provided by Project Gutenberg. Project Gutenberg is a non-profit organization founded by Michael Hart in 1971 at the University of Illinois. The mission of Project Gutenberg is simple: To encourage the creation and distribution of eBooks. Project Gutenberg is the first and largest collection of public domain eBooks.

Echoes from the Sabine Farm

Eugene Field

Imprint

This book is part of TREDITION CLASSICS

Author: Eugene Field
Cover design: Buchgut, Berlin – Germany

Publisher: tredition GmbH, Hamburg - Germany
ISBN: 978-3-8424-7440-6

www.tredition.com
www.tredition.de

The intention of the TREDITION CLASSICS series is to make world literature in the public domain available in printed format. Literary enthusiasts and organizations, such as Project Gutenberg, worldwide have scanned and digitally edited the original texts. tredition has subsequently formatted and redesigned the content into a modern reading layout. Therefore, we cannot guarantee the exact reproduction of the original format of a particular historic edition. Please also note that no modifications have been made to the spelling, therefore it may differ from the orthography used today.

THE WRITINGS IN PROSE AND VERSE OF EUGENE FIELD

ECHOES FROM THE SABINE FARM

by

Roswell Martin Field and Eugene Field

1899

INTRODUCTION

One Sunday evening in the winter of 1890 Eugene Field and the writer were walking in Lake View, Chicago, on their way to visit the library of a common friend, when the subject of publishing a book for Field came up for discussion.

The Little Book of Western Verse and The Little Book of Profitable Tales had been privately printed the year before at Chicago, and Field had been frequently reminded that the writer was ready and willing to stand sponsor for any new volume he, Field, might desire to bring out.

"The only thing I have on hand that might make a book," said Field, "are some few paraphrases of the Odes of Horace which my brother, 'Rose,' and I have been fooling over, and which, truth to tell, are certainly freely rendered. There are not enough of them, but we'll do some more, and I'll add a brief Life of Horace as a preface or introduction."

It is to be regretted that Field never carried out his intention with respect to this last, for he had given much thought and study to the great Roman satirist, and what Eugene Field could have said upon the subject must have been of interest. It is my belief that as he thought upon the matter it grew too great for him to handle within the space he had at first determined, and that tucked away within the recesses of his literary intentions was the determination, nullified by his early death, to write, *con amore*, a life of Quintus Horatius Flaccus.

This determination to write separately an extended account of Horace greatly reduced the bulk of the material intended for the Sabine Echoes, and it was with respect to this that Field apologetically and, as was his wont, humorously wrote:

"The volume may be rather thin *in corpore*, but think how hefty it will be intellectually."

When it came to the discussion of how many copies should be printed it was suggested that the edition be an exceedingly limited one, in order to cause as much scrambling and heartburning as possible among our bibliophilic brethren. And never shall I forget the seriousness of the man's face, nor the roars of laughter that followed, when he suggested that fifty copies only should be made, and that we should reserve one each and burn the other forty-eight!

It was a biting cold night and we had been loitering by the way, stopping to debate each point as it arose—but now we plunged on with excess of motion to keep ourselves warm, breaking out with occasional peals of laughter as we thought of our plan to make the publication what the booksellers call "excessively rare."

Field, elsewhere, has said he did not know why the original intention as to the destruction of the forty-eight copies was not carried out, but the answer is not far away. As the time for publication approached it was found impossible that such and such a friend should be forgotten in the matter of a copy, and so it went on until it was deemed prudent to add fifty to the number originally intended to be issued, and that decision, in the light of what followed, proved to be an eminently wise one. More than once some to me unknown friend of Field would write a pleasant lie as a reason to gain possession of the book, and up in a corner of the letter would be found an endorsement of the request after this fashion:

What's writ below
I'd have you know
Nor falsehood nor romance is;
It's solemn truth,
So grant the youth
The boon he seeks, dear Francis.

EUGENE FIELD.

It is perhaps unnecessary to add that, however flimsy the pretext upon which the request for a copy was made, it never failed of its object if it brought with it Field's endorsement. Among many pleasant utterances on this subject Field has said that but for the writer the Horatian verses would not have been given to the world—and this has been taken to mean more than was intended, and much unearned praise has been bestowed. But, in allusion to the original issue of the Odes, Field added, "in this charming guise," which places quite another construction upon the matter.

It may be that the enthusiasm displayed not only pleased Field, and incited him and his brother Roswell to perform that which, otherwise, might have been indefinitely deferred, but there is no question but that they intended to publish the Horatian odes at some time or another. Field was greatly delighted with the reception of this work, and I once heard him say it would outlive all his other books. He came naturally by his love of the classics. His father was a splendid scholar who obliged his sons to correspond with him in Latin. Field's favorite ode was the Bandusian Spring, the paraphrasing of which in the styles of the various writers of different periods gave him genuine joy and is perhaps the choice bit of the collection. The Echoes from the Sabine Farm was the most ambitious work Field had attempted up to the time of its issue. He was not at all sure that the public for whom he wrote, what following he then felt was his own, would accept his efforts in this direction with any sort of acclaim. Unquestionably, Field, at all times, believed in himself and in his power ultimately to make a name, as every man must who achieves success, but he was as far from believing that the public would accept him as an interpreter of Horatian odes as was Edward Fitzgerald with respect to Omar Khayyám. In short, he looked upon his work in the original publication of Echoes from the Sabine Farm as a labor of love—an effort from which some reputation might come, but certainly no monetary remuneration. It was because he so regarded it that he permitted the work to be first issued under the bolstering influence of a patron. It was, so he thought, an excellent opportunity to show his friends and acquaintances that his Pegasus was capable of soaring to classic heights, and he little dreamed that the paraphrasing of the Odes of Horace over which "Rose and I have been fooling" would be required for a *popular* edition. With the announcement of the Scribner edition of The Sabine Echoes came also the intelligence of Field's death.

I have found people who were somewhat puzzled as to the exact intentions of the Fields with respect to these translations and paraphrases. However, there can be no chance for mistake even to the veriest embryonic reader of Horace, if he will but remember that, while some of these transcriptions are indeed very faithful reproductions or adaptations of the original, others again are to be accepted as the very riot of burlesque verse-making.

The last stanza in the epilogue of this book reads:

Or if we part to meet no more
This side the misty Stygian river,
Be sure of this: On yonder shore
Sweet cheer awaiteth such as we—
A Sabine pagan's heaven, O friend—
And fellowship that knows no end.

FRANCIS WILSON.

January 22, 1896.

TO M.L. GRAY.

Come, dear old friend, and with us twain
To calm Digentian groves repair;
The turtle coos his sweet refrain
And posies are a-blooming there;
And there the romping Sabine girls
Bind myrtle in their lustrous curls.
I know a certain ilex-tree
Whence leaps a fountain cool and clear.
Its voices summon you and me;
Come, let us haste to share its cheer!
Methinks the rapturous song it sings
Should woo our thoughts from mortal things.
But, good old friend, I charge thee well,
Watch thou my brother all the while,
Lest some fair Lydia cast her spell
Round him unschooled in female guile.
Those damsels have no charms for me;
Guard thou that brother,—I'll guard thee!
And, lo, sweet friend! behold this cup,
Round which the garlands intertwine;
With Massic it is foaming up,
And we would drink to thee and thine.
And of the draught thou shalt partake,
Who lov'st us for our father's sake.

Hark you! from yonder Sabine farm
Echo the songs of long ago,
With power to soothe and grace to charm
What ills humanity may know;
With that sweet music in the air,
'T is Love and Summer everywhere.
So, though no grief consumes our lot
(Since all our lives have been discreet),
Come, in this consecrated spot,
Let's see if pagan cheer be sweet.
Now, then, the songs; but, first, more wine.
The gods be with you, friends of mine!

E.F.

The Contents of this Book

WRITTEN IN COLLABORATION WITH ROSWELL MARTIN FIELD

FAME *vs.* RICHES.	Ars Poetica, line 323	E.F.
THE LYRIC MUSE.	Ars Poetica, line 301	E.F.
A COUNTERBLAST AGAINST GAR-LIC.	Epode III.	R.M.F.
AN EXCUSE FOR LALAGE.	Odes, II. 5	R.M.F.
AN APPEAL TO LYCE.	Odes, IV. 13	R.M.F.
A ROMAN WINTER-PIECE I.	Odes, I. 9	E.F.
A ROMAN WINTER-PIECE II.		R.M.F.
TO DIANA.	Odes, III. 22	R.M.F.
TO HIS LUTE.	Odes, I. 32	E.F.
TO LEUCONÖE I.	Odes, I. 11	R.M.F.
TO LEUCONÖE II.		E.F.
TO LIGURINUS I.	Odes, IV. 10	R.M.F.
TO LIGURINUS II.		E.F.
THE HAPPY ISLES.	Epode XIV. line 41	E.F.
CONSISTENCY.	Ars Poetica	E.F.
TO POSTUMUS.	Odes, II. 14	R.M.F.
TO MISTRESS PYRRHA I.	Odes, I. 5	E.F.
TO MISTRESS PYRRHA II.		R.M.F.
TO MELPOMENE.	Odes, III. 30	E.F.
TO PHYLLIS I.	Odes, IV. 11.	E.F.

IN THE SPRINGTIME. I.	Odes, I. 4	E.F.
IN THE SPRINGTIME. II.		R.M.F.
TO A BULLY.	Epode VI.	E.F.
TO MOTHER VENUS.		
TO LYDIA.	Odes, I. 8	E.F.
TO NEOBULE.	Odes, III. 12	R.M.F.
AT THE BALL GAME.	Odes, V. 17.	R.M.F.
EPILOGUE.		E.F.

Echoes from the Sabine Farm

AN INVITATION TO MÆCENAS

Dear, noble friend! a virgin cask
Of wine solicits your attention;
And roses fair, to deck your hair,
And things too numerous to mention.
So tear yourself awhile away
From urban turmoil, pride, and splendor,
And deign to share what humble fare
And sumptuous fellowship I tender.
The sweet content retirement brings
Smoothes out the ruffled front of kings.

The evil planets have combined
To make the weather hot and hotter;
By parboiled streams the shepherd dreams
Vainly of ice-cream soda-water.
And meanwhile you, defying heat,
With patriotic ardor ponder
On what old Rome essays at home,
And what her heathen do out yonder.
Mæcenas, no such vain alarm
Disturbs the quiet of this farm!

God in His providence obscures
The goal beyond this vale of sorrow,
And smiles at men in pity when
They seek to penetrate the morrow.
With faith that all is for the best,
Let's bear what burdens are presented,
That we shall say, let come what may,
"We die, as we have lived, contented!
Ours is to-day; God's is the rest,—
He doth ordain who knoweth best."

Dame Fortune plays me many a prank.

When she is kind, oh, how I go it!
But if again she's harsh,—why, then
I am a very proper poet!
When favoring gales bring in my ships,
I hie to Rome and live in clover;
Elsewise I steer my skiff out here,
And anchor till the storm blows over.
Compulsory virtue is the charm
Of life upon the Sabine farm!

CHLORIS PROPERLY REBUKED

Chloris, my friend, I pray you your misconduct to forswear;
The wife of poor old Ibycus should have more *savoir faire*.
A woman at your time of life, and drawing near death's door,
Should not play with the girly girls, and think she's *en rapport*.

What's good enough for Pholoe you cannot well essay;
Your daughter very properly courts *the jeunesse dorée*,—
A Thyiad, who, when timbrel beats, cannot her joy restrain,
But plays the kid, and laughs and giggles *à l'Américaine*.

'T is more becoming, Madame, in a creature old and poor,
To sit and spin than to engage in an *affaire d'amour*.
The lutes, the roses, and the wine drained deep are not for you;
Remember what the poet says: *Ce monde est plein de fous!*

TO THE FOUNTAIN OF BANDUSIA

O fountain of Bandusia!
Whence crystal waters flow,
With garlands gay and wine I'll pay
The sacrifice I owe;
A sportive kid with budding horns
I have, whose crimson blood
Anon shall dye and sanctify

Thy cool and babbling flood.

O fountain of Bandusia!
The Dog-star's hateful spell
No evil brings into the springs
That from thy bosom well;
Here oxen, wearied by the plow,
The roving cattle here
Hasten in quest of certain rest,
And quaff thy gracious cheer.

O fountain of Bandusia!
Ennobled shalt thou be,
For I shall sing the joys that spring
Beneath yon ilex-tree.
Yes, fountain of Bandusia,
Posterity shall know
The cooling brooks that from thy nooks
Singing and dancing go.

TO THE FOUNTAIN OF BANDUSIA

O fountain of Bandusia! more glittering than glass,
And worthy of the pleasant wine and toasts that freely pass;
More worthy of the flowers with which thou modestly art hid,
To-morrow willing hands shall sacrifice to thee a kid.

In vain the glory of the brow where proudly swell above
The growing horns, significant of battle and of love;
For in thy honor he shall die, – the offspring of the herd, –
And with his crimson life-blood thy cold waters shall be stirred.

The Dog-star's cruel season, with its fierce and blazing heat,
Has never sent its scorching rays into thy glad retreat;
The oxen, wearied with the plow, the herd which wanders near,
Have found a grateful respite and delicious coolness here.

When of the graceful ilex on the hollow rocks I sing,
Thou shalt become illustrious, O sweet Bandusian spring!
Among the noble fountains which have been enshrined in fame,
Thy dancing, babbling waters shall in song our homage claim.

THE PREFERENCE DECLARED

Boy, I detest the Persian pomp;
I hate those linden-bark devices;
And as for roses, holy Moses!
They can't be got at living prices!
Myrtle is good enough for us,—
For *you*, as bearer of my flagon;
For *me*, supine beneath this vine,
Doing my best to get a jag on!

A TARDY APOLOGY

I

Mæcenas, you will be my death,—though friendly you profess yourself,—
If to me in a strain like this so often you address yourself:
"Come, Holly, why this laziness? Why indolently shock you us?
Why with Lethean cups fall into desuetude innocuous?"

A god, Mæcenas! yea, a god hath proved the very curse of me!
If my iambics are not done, pray, do not think the worse of me;
Anacreon for young Bathyllus burned without apology,
And wept his simple measures on a sample of conchology.

Now, you yourself, Mæcenas, are enjoying this beatitude;
If by no brighter beauty Ilium fell, you've cause for gratitude.
A certain Phryne keeps me on the rack with lovers numerous;
This is the artful hussy's neat conception of the humorous!

A TARDY APOLOGY

II

You ask me, friend,
Why I don't send
The long since due-and-paid-for numbers;
Why, songless, I
As drunken lie
Abandoned to Lethean slumbers.

Long time ago
(As well you know)
I started in upon that carmen;

My work was vain,—
But why complain?
When gods forbid, how helpless are men!

Some ages back,
The sage Anack
Courted a frisky Samian body,
Singing her praise
In metered phrase
As flowing as his bowls of toddy.

Till I was hoarse
Might I discourse
Upon the cruelties of Venus;
'T were waste of time
As well of rhyme,
For you've been there yourself, Mæcenas!

Perfect your bliss
If some fair miss
Love you yourself and *not* your minæ;
I, fortune's sport,
All vainly court
The beauteous, polyandrous Phryne!

TO THE SHIP OF STATE

O ship of state
Shall new winds bear you back upon the sea?
What are you doing? Seek the harbor's lee
Ere 't is too late!

Do you bemoan
Your side was stripped of oarage in the blast?
Swift Africus has weakened, too, your mast;
The sailyards groan.

Of cables bare,

Your keel can scarce endure the lordly wave.
Your sails are rent; you have no gods to save,
Or answer pray'r.

Though Pontic pine,
The noble daughter of a far-famed wood,
You boast your lineage and title good,—
A useless line!

The sailor there
In painted sterns no reassurance finds;
Unless you owe derision to the winds,
Beware—beware!

My grief erewhile,
But now my care—my longing! shun the seas
That flow between the gleaming Cyclades,
Each shining isle.

QUITTING AGAIN

The hero of
Affairs of love
By far too numerous to be mentioned,
And scarred as I'm,
It seemeth time
That I were mustered out and pensioned.

So on this wall
My lute and all
I hang, and dedicate to Venus;
And I implore
But one thing more
Ere all is at an end between us.

O goddess fair
Who reignest where
The weather's seldom bleak and snowy,

This boon I urge:
In anger scourge
My old cantankerous sweetheart, Chloe!

SAILOR AND SHADE

SAILOR

You, who have compassed land and sea,
Now all unburied lie;
All vain your store of human lore,
For you were doomed to die.
The sire of Pelops likewise fell,—
Jove's honored mortal guest;
So king and sage of every age
At last lie down to rest.
Plutonian shades enfold the ghost
Of that majestic one
Who taught as truth that he, forsooth,
Had once been Pentheus' son;
Believe who may, he's passed away,
And what he did is done.
A last night comes alike to all;
One path we all must tread,
Through sore disease or stormy seas
Or fields with corpses red.
Whate'er our deeds, that pathway leads
To regions of the dead.

SHADE

The fickle twin Illyrian gales
Overwhelmed me on the wave;
But you that live, I pray you give
My bleaching bones a grave!
Oh, then when cruel tempests rage
You all unharmed shall be;
Jove's mighty hand shall guard by land
And Neptune's on the sea.
Perchance you fear to do what may
Bring evil to your race?
Oh, rather fear that like me here
You'll lack a burial place.

So, though you be in proper haste,
Bide long enough, I pray,
To give me, friend, what boon shall send
My soul upon its way!

LET US HAVE PEACE

In maudlin spite let Thracians fight
Above their bowls of liquor;
But such as we, when on a spree,
Should never brawl and bicker!

These angry words and clashing swords
Are quite *de trop*, I'm thinking;
Brace up, my boys, and hush your noise,
And drown your wrath in drinking.

Aha, 't is fine,—this mellow wine
With which our host would dope us!
Now let us hear what pretty dear
Entangles him of Opus.

I see you blush,—nay, comrades, hush!
Come, friend, though they despise you,
Tell me the name of that fair dame,—
Perchance I may advise you.

O wretched youth! and is it truth
You love that fickle lady?
I, doting dunce, courted her once;
Since when, she's reckoned shady!

TO QUINTUS DELLIUS

Be tranquil, Dellius, I pray;
For though you pine your life away
With dull complaining breath,
Or speed with song and wine each day,

Still, still your doom is death.

Where the white poplar and the pine
In glorious arching shade combine,
And the brook singing goes,
Bid them bring store of nard and wine
And garlands of the rose.

Let's live while chance and youth obtain;
Soon shall you quit this fair domain
Kissed by the Tiber's gold,
And all your earthly pride and gain
Some heedless heir shall hold.

One ghostly boat shall some time bear
From scenes of mirthfulness or care
Each fated human soul,—
Shall waft and leave its burden where
The waves of Lethe roll.

So come, I prithee, Dellius mine;
Let's sing our songs and drink our wine
In that sequestered nook
Where the white poplar and the pine
Stand listening to the brook.

POKING FUN AT XANTHIAS

Of your love for your handmaid you need feel no shame.
Don't apologize, Xanthias, pray;
Remember, Achilles the proud felt a flame
For Brissy, his slave, as they say.
Old Telamon's son, fiery Ajax, was moved
By the captive Tecmessa's ripe charms;
And Atrides, suspending the feast, it behooved
To gather a girl to his arms.

Now, how do you know that this yellow-haired maid
(This Phyllis you fain would enjoy)
Hasn't parents whose wealth would cast you in the shade,—

Who would ornament you, Xan, my boy?
Very likely the poor chick sheds copious tears,
And is bitterly thinking the while
Of the royal good times of her earlier years,
When her folks regulated the style!

It won't do at all, my dear boy, to believe
That she of whose charms you are proud
Is beautiful only as means to deceive,—
Merely one of the horrible crowd.
So constant a sweetheart, so loving a wife,
So averse to all notions of greed
Was surely not born of a mother whose life
Is a chapter you'd better not read.

As an unbiased party I feel it my place
(For I don't like to do things by halves)
To compliment Phyllis,—her arms and her face
And (excuse me!) her delicate calves.
Tut, tut! don't get angry, my boy, or suspect
You have any occasion to fear
A man whose deportment is always correct,
And is now in his forty-first year!

TO ARISTIUS FUSCUS

Fuscus, whoso to good inclines,
And is a faultless liver,
Nor Moorish spear nor bow need fear,
Nor poison-arrowed quiver.

Ay, though through desert wastes he roam,
Or scale the rugged mountains,
Or rest beside the murmuring tide
Of weird Hydaspan fountains!

Lo, on a time, I gayly paced
The Sabine confines shady,

And sung in glee of Lalage,
My own and dearest lady;

And as I sung, a monster wolf
Slunk through the thicket from me;
But for that song, as I strolled along,
He would have overcome me!

Set me amid those poison mists
Which no fair gale dispelleth,
Or in the plains where silence reigns,
And no thing human dwelleth,—

Still shall I love my Lalage,
Still sing her tender graces;
And while I sing, my theme shall bring
Heaven to those desert places!

TO ALBIUS TIBULLUS

I

Not to lament that rival flame
Wherewith the heartless Glycera scorns you,
Nor waste your time in maudlin rhyme,
How many a modern instance warns you!

Fair-browed Lycoris pines away
Because her Cyrus loves another;
The ruthless churl informs the girl
He loves her only as a brother!

For he, in turn, courts Pholoe,—
A maid unscotched of love's fierce virus;
Why, goats will mate with wolves they hate
Ere Pholoe will mate with Cyrus!

Ah, weak and hapless human hearts,
By cruel Mother Venus fated
To spend this life in hopeless strife,
Because incongruously mated!

Such torture, Albius, is my lot;
For, though a better mistress wooed me,
My Myrtale has captured me,
And with her cruelties subdued me!

TO ALBIUS TIBULLUS

II

Grieve not, my Albius, if thoughts of Glycera may haunt you,
Nor chant your mournful elegies because she faithless proves;
If now a younger man than you this cruel charmer loves,
Let not the kindly favors of the past rise up to taunt you.

Lycoris of the little brow for Cyrus feels a passion,
And Cyrus, on the other hand, toward Pholoe inclines;
But ere this crafty Cyrus can accomplish his designs
She-goats will wed Apulian wolves in deference to fashion.

Such is the will, the cruel will, of love-inciting Venus,
Who takes delight in wanton sport and ill-considered jokes,
And brings ridiculous misfits beneath her brazen yokes,—
A very infelicitous proceeding, just between us.

As for myself, young Myrtale, slave-born and lacking graces,
And wilder than the Adrian tides which form Calabrian bays,
Entangled me in pleasing chains and compromising ways,
When—just my luck—a better girl was courting my embraces.

TO MÆCENAS

Mæcenas, thou of royalty's descent,
Both my protector and dear ornament,
Among humanity's conditions are
Those who take pleasure in the flying car,
Whirling Olympian dust, as on they roll,
And shunning with the glowing wheel the goal;
While the ennobling palm, the prize of worth,
Exalts them to the gods, the lords of earth.

Here one is happy if the fickle crowd
His name the threefold honor has allowed;
And there another, if into his stores
Comes what is swept from Libyan threshing-floors.

He who delights to till his father's lands,
And grasps the delving-hoe with willing hands,
Can never to Attalic offers hark,
Or cut the Myrtoan Sea with Cyprian bark.
The merchant, timorous of Afric's breeze,
When fiercely struggling with Icarian seas
Praises the restful quiet of his home,
Nor wishes from the peaceful fields to roam;
Ah, speedily his shattered ships he mends,—
To poverty his lesson ne'er extends.

One there may be who never scorns to fill
His cups with mellow draughts from Massic's hill,
Nor from the busy day an hour to wean,
Now stretched at length beneath the arbute green,
Now at the softly whispering spring, to dream
Of the fair nymphs who haunt the sacred stream.
For camp and trump and clarion some have zest,—
The cruel wars the mothers so detest.
'Neath the cold sky the hunter spends his life,
Unmindful of his home and tender wife,
Whether the doe is seen by faithful hounds
Or Marsian boar through the fine meshes bounds.

But as for me, the ivy-wreaths, the prize
Of learned brows, exalt me to the skies;
The shady grove, the nymphs and satyrs there,
Draw me away from people everywhere;
If it may be, Euterpe's flute inspires,
Or Polyhymnia strikes the Lesbian lyres;
And if you place me where no bard debars,
With head exalted I shall strike the stars!

TO HIS BOOK

You vain, self-conscious little book,
Companion of my happy days,
How eagerly you seem to look
For wider fields to spread your lays;

My desk and locks cannot contain you,
Nor blush of modesty restrain you.

Well, then, begone, fool that thou art!
But do not come to me and cry,
When critics strike you to the heart:
"Oh, wretched little book am I!"
You know I tried to educate you
To shun the fate that must await you.

In youth you may encounter friends
(Pray this prediction be not wrong),
But wait until old age descends
And thumbs have smeared your gentlest song;
Then will the moths connive to eat you
And rural libraries secrete you.

However, should a friend some word
Of my obscure career request,
Tell him how deeply I was stirred
To spread my wings beyond the nest;
Take from my years, which are before you,
To boom my merits, I implore you.

Tell him that I am short and fat,
Quick in my temper, soon appeased,
With locks of gray,—but what of that?
Loving the sun, with nature pleased.
I'm more than four and forty, hark you,—
But ready for a night off, mark you!

FAME *vs.* RICHES

The Greeks had genius,—'t was a gift
The Muse vouchsafed in glorious measure;
The boon of Fame they made their aim
And prized above all worldly treasure.

But *we*,—how do we train *our* youth?
Not in the arts that are immortal,
But in the greed for gains that speed
From him who stands at Death's dark portal.

Ah, when this slavish love of gold
Once binds the soul in greasy fetters,
How prostrate lies,—how droops and dies
The great, the noble cause of letters!

THE LYRIC MUSE

I love the lyric muse!
For when mankind ran wild in grooves
Came holy Orpheus with his songs
And turned men's hearts from bestial loves,
From brutal force and savage wrongs;
Amphion, too, and on his lyre
Made such sweet music all the day
That rocks, instinct with warm desire,
Pursued him in his glorious way.

I love the lyric muse!
Hers was the wisdom that of yore
Taught man the rights of fellow man,
Taught him to worship God the more,
And to revere love's holy ban.
Hers was the hand that jotted down
The laws correcting divers wrongs;
And so came honor and renown
To bards and to their noble songs.

I love the lyric muse!
Old Homer sung unto the lyre;
Tyrtæus, too, in ancient days;
Still warmed by their immortal fire,
How doth our patriot spirit blaze!
The oracle, when questioned, sings;

So our first steps in life are taught.
In verse we soothe the pride of kings,
In verse the drama has been wrought.

I love the lyric muse!
Be not ashamed, O noble friend,
In honest gratitude to pay
Thy homage to the gods that send
This boon to charm all ill away.
With solemn tenderness revere
This voiceful glory as a shrine
Wherein the quickened heart may hear
The counsels of a voice divine!

A COUNTERBLAST AGAINST GARLIC

May the man who has cruelly murdered his sire –
A crime to be punished with death –
Be condemned to eat garlic till he shall expire
Of his own foul and venomous breath!
What stomachs these rustics must have who can eat
This dish that Canidia made,
Which imparts to my colon a torturous heat,
And a poisonous look, I'm afraid!

They say that ere Jason attempted to yoke
The fire-breathing bulls to the plow
He smeared his whole body with garlic, – a joke
Which I fully appreciate now.
When Medea gave Glauce her beautiful dress,
In which garlic was scattered about,
It was cruel and rather low-down, I confess,
But it settled the point beyond doubt.

On thirsty Apulia ne'er has the sun
Inflicted such terrible heat;
As for Hercules' robe, although poisoned, 't was fun
When compared with this garlic we eat!

Mæcenas, if ever on garbage like this
You express a desire to be fed,
May Mrs. Mæcenas object to your kiss,
And lie at the foot of the bed!

AN EXCUSE FOR LALAGE

To bear the yoke not yet your love's submissive neck is bent,
To share a husband's toil, or grasp his amorous intent;
Over the fields, in cooling streams, the heifer longs to go,
Now with the calves disporting where the pussy-willows grow.

Give up your thirst for unripe grapes, and, trust me, you shall learn
How quickly in the autumn time to purple they will turn.
Soon she will follow you, for age steals swiftly on the maid;
And all the precious years that you have lost she will have paid.

Soon she will seek a lord, beloved as Pholoe, the coy,
Or Chloris, or young Gyges, that deceitful, girlish boy,
Whom, if you placed among the girls, and loosed his flowing locks,
The wondering guests could not decide which one decorum shocks.

AN APPEAL TO LYCE

Lyce, the gods have heard my prayers, as gods will hear the dutiful,
And brought old age upon you, though you still affect the beautiful.
You sport among the boys, and drink and chatter on quite aimlessly;
And in your cups with quavering voice you torment Cupid shamelessly.

For blooming Chia, Cupid has a feeling more than brotherly;
He knows a handsaw from a hawk whenever winds are southerly.
He pats her pretty cheeks, but looks on you as a monstrosity;
Your wrinkles and your yellow teeth excite his animosity.

For jewels bright and purple Coan robes you are not dressable;
Unhappily for you, the public records are accessible.
Where is your charm, and where your bloom and gait so firm and sensible,

That drew my love from Cinara,—a lapse most indefensible?

To my poor Cinara in youth Death came with great celerity;
Egad, that never can be said of you with any verity!
The old crow that you are, the teasing boys will jeer, compelling you
To roost at home. Reflect, all this is straight that I am telling you.

A ROMAN WINTER-PIECE

I

See, Thaliarch mine, how, white with snow,
Soracte mocks the sullen sky;
How, groaning loud, the woods are bowed,
And chained with frost the rivers lie.

Pile, pile the logs upon the hearth;
We'll melt away the envious cold:
And, better yet, sweet friend, we'll wet
Our whistles with some four-year-old.

Commit all else unto the gods,
Who, when it pleaseth them, shall bring
To fretful deeps and wooded steeps
The mild, persuasive grace of Spring.

Let not To-morrow, but To-day,
Your ever active thoughts engage;
Frisk, dance, and sing, and have your fling,
Unharmed, unawed of crabbed Age.

Let's steal content from Winter's wrath,
And glory in the artful theft,
That years from now folks shall allow
'T was cold indeed when we got left.

So where the whisperings and the mirth
Of girls invite a sportive chap,
Let's fare awhile,—aha, you smile;
You guess my meaning,—*verbum sap*.

A ROMAN WINTER-PIECE

II

Now stands Soracte white with snow, now bend the laboring trees,
And with the sharpness of the frost the stagnant rivers freeze.
Pile up the billets on the hearth, to warmer cheer incline,
And draw, my Thaliarchus, from the Sabine jar the wine.

The rest leave to the gods, who still the fiercely warring wind,
And to the morrow's store of good or evil give no mind.
Whatever day your fortune grants, that day mark up for gain;
And in your youthful bloom do not the sweet amours disdain.

Now on the Campus and the squares, when evening shades descend,
Soft whisperings again are heard, and loving voices blend;
And now the low delightful laugh betrays the lurking maid,
While from her slowly yielding arms the forfeiture is paid.

TO DIANA

O virgin, tri-formed goddess fair,
The guardian of the groves and hills,
Who hears the girls in their despair
Cry out in childbirth's cruel ills,
And saves them from the Stygian flow!
Let the pine-tree my cottage near
Be sacred to thee evermore,
That I may give to it each year
With joy the life-blood of the boar,
Now thinking of the sidelong blow.

TO HIS LUTE

If ever in the sylvan shade
A song immortal we have made,
Come now, O lute, I prithee come,
Inspire a song of Latium!

A Lesbian first thy glories proved;
In arms and in repose he loved
To sweep thy dulcet strings, and raise
His voice in Love's and Liber's praise.
The Muses, too, and him who clings
To Mother Venus' apron-strings,
And Lycus beautiful, he sung
In those old days when you were young.

O shell, that art the ornament
Of Phoebus, bringing sweet content
To Jove, and soothing troubles all, —
Come and requite me, when I call!

TO LEUCONÖE

I

What end the gods may have ordained for me,
And what for thee,
Seek not to learn, Leuconöe; we may not know.
Chaldean tables cannot bring us rest.
'T is for the best
To bear in patience what may come, or weal or woe.

If for more winters our poor lot is cast,
Or this the last,
Which on the crumbling rocks has dashed Etruscan seas,
Strain clear the wine; this life is short, at best.
Take hope with zest,
And, trusting not To-morrow, snatch To-day for ease!

TO LEUCONÖE

II

Seek not, Leuconöe, to know how long you're going to live yet,
What boons the gods will yet withhold, or what they're going to give yet;
For Jupiter will have his way, despite how much we worry,—
Some will hang on for many a day, and some die in a hurry.
The wisest thing for you to do is to embark this diem
Upon a merry escapade with some such bard as I am.
And while we sport I'll reel you off such odes as shall surprise ye;
To-morrow, when the headache comes,—well, then I'll satirize ye!

TO LIGURINUS

I

Though mighty in Love's favor still,
Though cruel yet, my boy,
When the unwelcome dawn shall chill
Your pride and youthful joy,
The hair which round your shoulder grows
Is rudely cut away,
Your color, redder than the rose,
Is changed by youth's decay,—

Then, Ligurinus, in the glass
Another you will spy.
And as the shaggy face, alas!
You see, your grief will cry:
"Why in my youth could I not learn
The wisdom men enjoy?
Or why to men cannot return
The smooth cheeks of the boy?"

TO LIGURINUS

II

O Cruel fair,
Whose flowing hair
The envy and the pride of all is,
As onward roll
The years, that poll
Will get as bald as a billiard ball is;
Then shall your skin, now pink and dimply,
Be tanned to parchment, sear and pimply!

When you behold
Yourself grown old,
These words shall speak your spirits moody:
"Unhappy one!
What heaps of fun
I've missed by being goody-goody!
Oh, that I might have felt the hunger
Of loveless age when I was younger!"

THE HAPPY ISLES

Oh, come with me to the Happy Isles
In the golden haze off yonder,
Where the song of the sun-kissed breeze beguiles
And the ocean loves to wander.

Fragrant the vines that mantle those hills,
Proudly the fig rejoices,
Merrily dance the virgin rills,
Blending their myriad voices.

Our herds shall suffer no evil there,
But peacefully feed and rest them;
Never thereto shall prowling bear
Or serpent come to molest them.

Neither shall Eurus, wanton bold,
Nor feverish drought distress us,
But he that compasseth heat and cold
Shall temper them both to bless us.

There no vandal foot has trod,
And the pirate hordes that wander
Shall never profane the sacred sod
Of those beautiful isles out yonder.

Never a spell shall blight our vines,
Nor Sirius blaze above us,
But you and I shall drink our wines
And sing to the loved that love us.

So come with me where Fortune smiles
And the gods invite devotion,—
Oh, come with me to the Happy Isles
In the haze of that far-off ocean!

CONSISTENCY

Should painter attach to a fair human head
The thick, turgid neck of a stallion,
Or depict a spruce lass with the tail of a bass,
I am sure you would guy the rapscallion.

Believe me, dear Pisos, that just such a freak
Is the crude and preposterous poem
Which merely abounds in a torrent of sounds,
With no depth of reason below 'em.

'T is all very well to give license to art,—
The wisdom of license defend I;
But the line should be drawn at the fripperish spawn
Of a mere *cacoethes scribendi*.

It is too much the fashion to strain at effects,—

Yes, that's what's the matter with Hannah!
Our popular taste, by the tyros debased,
Paints each barnyard a grove of Diana!

Should a patron require you to paint a marine,
Would you work in some trees with their barks on?
When his strict orders are for a Japanese jar,
Would you give him a pitcher like Clarkson?

Now, this is my moral: Compose what you may,
And Fame will be ever far distant
Unless you combine with a simple design
A treatment in toto consistent.

TO POSTUMUS

O Postumus, my Postumus, the years are gliding past,
And piety will never check the wrinkles coming fast,
The ravages of time old age's swift advance has made,
And death, which unimpeded comes to bear us to the shade.

Old friend, although the tearless Pluto you may strive to please,
And seek each year with thrice one hundred bullocks to appease,
Who keeps the thrice-huge Geryon and Tityus his slaves,
Imprisoned fast forevermore with cold and sombre waves,

Yet must that flood so terrible be sailed by mortals all;
Whether perchance we may be kings and live in royal hall,
Or lowly peasants struggling long with poverty and dearth,
Still must we cross who live upon the favors of the earth.

And all in vain from bloody war and contest we are free,
And from the waves that hoarsely break upon the Adrian Sea;
For our frail bodies all in vain our helpless terror grows
In gloomy autumn seasons, when the baneful south wind blows.

Alas! the black Cocytus, wandering to the world below,
That languid river to behold we of this earth must go;
To see the grim Danaides, that miserable race,
And Sisyphus of Æolus, condemned to endless chase.

Behind you must you leave your home and land and wife so dear,
And of the trees, except the hated cypresses, you rear,
And which around the funeral piles as signs of mourning grow,
Not one will follow you, their short-lived master, there below.

Your worthier heir the precious Cæcuban shall drink galore,
Now with a hundred keys preserved and guarded in your store,
And stain the pavements, pouring out in waste the nectar proud,
Better than that with which the pontiffs' feasts have been endowed.

TO MISTRESS PYRRHA

I

What perfumed, posie-dizened sirrah,
With smiles for diet,
Clasps you, O fair but faithless Pyrrha,
On the quiet?
For whom do you bind up your tresses,
As spun-gold yellow,—
Meshes that go with your caresses,
To snare a fellow?

How will he rail at fate capricious,
And curse you duly,
Yet now he deems your wiles delicious,—
You perfect, truly!
Pyrrha, your love's a treacherous ocean;
He'll soon fall in there!
Then shall I gloat on his commotion,
For *I* have been there!

TO MISTRESS PYRRHA

II

What dainty boy with sweet perfumes bedewed
Has lavished kisses, Pyrrha, in the cave?
For whom amid the roses, many-hued,
Do you bind back your tresses' yellow wave?

How oft will he deplore your fickle whim,
And wonder at the storm and roughening deeps,
Who now enjoys you, all in all to him,
And dreams of you, whose only thoughts he keeps.

Wretched are they to whom you seem so fair;—
That I escaped the storms, the gods be praised!
My dripping garments, offered with a prayer,
Stand as a tablet to the sea-god raised.

TO MELPOMENE

Lofty and enduring is the monument I've reared:
Come, tempests, with your bitterness assailing;
And thou, corrosive blasts of time, by all things mortal feared,
Thy buffets and thy rage are unavailing!

I shall not altogether die: by far my greater part
Shall mock man's common fate in realms infernal;
My works shall live as tributes to my genius and my art,—
My works shall be my monument eternal!

While this great Roman empire stands and gods protect our fanes,
Mankind with grateful hearts shall tell the story
How one most lowly born upon the parched Apulian plains
First raised the native lyric muse to glory.

Assume, revered Melpomene, the proud estate I've won,
And, with thine own dear hand the meed supplying,
Bind thou about the forehead of thy celebrated son
The Delphic laurel-wreath of fame undying!

TO PHYLLIS

I

Come, Phyllis, I've a cask of wine
That fairly reeks with precious juices,
And in your tresses you shall twine
The loveliest flowers this vale produces.

My cottage wears a gracious smile;
The altar, decked in floral glory,
Yearns for the lamb which bleats the while
As though it pined for honors gory.

Hither our neighbors nimbly fare,
The boys agog, the maidens snickering;
And savory smells possess the air,
As skyward kitchen flames are flickering.

You ask what means this grand display,
This festive throng and goodly diet?
Well, since you're bound to have your way,
I don't mind telling, on the quiet.

'T is April 13, as you know,
A day and month devote to Venus,
Whereon was born, some years ago,
My very worthy friend, Mæcenas.

Nay, pay no heed to Telephus;
Your friends agree he doesn't love you.
The way he flirts convinces us
He really is not worthy of you.

Aurora's son, unhappy lad!
You know the fate that overtook him?
And Pegasus a rider had, —
I say he *had*, before he shook him!

Hoc docet (as you must agree)
'T is meet that Phyllis should discover
A wisdom in preferring me,
And mittening every other lover.

So come, O Phyllis, last and best
Of loves with which this heart's been smitten,
Come, sing my jealous fears to rest,
And let your songs be those *I've* written.

TO PHYLLIS

II

Sweet Phyllis, I have here a jar of old and precious wine,
The years which mark its coming from the Alban hills are nine,
And in the garden parsley, too, for wreathing garlands fair,
And ivy in profusion to bind up your shining hair.

Now smiles the house with silver; the altar, laurel-bound,
Longs with the sacrificial blood of lambs to drip around;
The company is hurrying, boys and maidens with the rest;
The flames are flickering as they whirl the dark smoke on their crest.

Yet you must know the joys to which you have been summoned here
To keep the Ides of April, to the sea-born Venus dear,—
Ah, festal day more sacred than my own fair day of birth,
Since from its dawn my loved Mæcenas counts his years of earth.

A rich and wanton girl has caught, as suited to her mind,
The Telephus whom you desire,—a youth not of your kind.
She holds him bound with pleasing chains, the fetters of her charms,—
Remember how scorched Phaëthon ambitious hopes alarms.

The winged Pegasus the rash Bellerophon has chafed,
To you a grave example for reflection has vouchsafed,—
Always to follow what is meet, and never try to catch
That which is not allowed to you, an inappropriate match.

Come now, sweet Phyllis, of my loves the last, and hence the best
(For nevermore shall other girls inflame this manly breast);
Learn loving measures to rehearse as we may stroll along,
And dismal cares shall fly away and vanish at your song.

TO CHLOE

I

Why do you shun me, Chloe, like the fawn,
That, fearful of the breezes and the wood,
Has sought her timorous mother since the dawn,
And on the pathless mountain tops has stood?

Her trembling heart a thousand fears invites,
Her sinking knees with nameless terrors shake,—
Whether the rustling leaf of spring affrights,
Or the green lizards stir the slumbering brake.

I do not follow with a tigerish thought,
Or with the fierce Gætulian lion's quest;
So, quickly leave your mother, as you ought,
Full ripe to nestle on a husband's breast.

TO CHLOE

II

Chloe, you shun me like a hind
That, seeking vainly for her mother,
Hears danger in each breath of wind,
And wildly darts this way and t' other;

Whether the breezes sway the wood
Or lizards scuttle through the brambles,
She starts, and off, as though pursued,
The foolish, frightened creature scrambles.

But, Chloe, you're no infant thing
That should esteem a man an ogre;
Let go your mother's apron-string,
And pin your faith upon a toga!

III

A PARAPHRASE

How happens it, my cruel miss,
You're always giving me the mitten?
You seem to have forgotten this:
That you no longer are a kitten!

A woman that has reached the years
Of that which people call discretion
Should put aside all childish fears
And see in courtship no transgression.

A mother's solace may be sweet,
But Hymen's tenderness is sweeter;
And though all virile love be meet,
You'll find the poet's love is metre.

IV

A PARAPHRASE, CIRCA 1715

Since Chloe is so monstrous fair,
With such an eye and such an air,
What wonder that the world complains
When she each am'rous suit disdains?

Close to her mother's side she clings,
And mocks the death her folly brings
To gentle swains that feel the smarts
Her eyes inflict upon their hearts.

Whilst thus the years of youth go by,
Shall Colin languish, Strephon die?
Nay, cruel nymph! come, choose a mate,
And choose him ere it be too late!

V

A PARAPHRASE, BY DR. I.W.

Why, Mistress Chloe, do you bother
With prattlings and with vain ado
Your worthy and industrious mother,
Eschewing them that come to woo?

Oh, that the awful truth might quicken
This stern conviction to your breast:
You are no longer now a chicken
Too young to quit the parent nest.

So put aside your froward carriage,
And fix your thoughts, whilst yet there's time,
Upon the righteousness of marriage
With some such godly man as I'm.

VI

A PARAPHRASE, BY CHAUCER

Syn that you, Chloe, to your moder sticken,
Maketh all ye yonge bacheloures full sicken;
Like as a lyttel deere you ben y-hiding
Whenas come lovers with theyre pityse chiding.
Sothly it ben faire to give up your moder
For to beare swete company with some oder;
Your moder ben well enow so farre shee goeth,
But that ben not farre enow, God knoweth;
Wherefore it ben sayed that foolysh ladyes
That marrye not shall leade an aype in Hadys;
But all that do with gode men wed full quicklye
When that they be on dead go to ye seints full sickerly.

TO MÆCENAS

Than you, O valued friend of mine,
A better patron *non est*!
Come, quaff my home-made Sabine wine,—
You'll find it poor but honest.

I put it up that famous day
You patronized the ballet,
And the public cheered you such a way
As shook your native valley.

Cæcuban and the Calean brand
May elsewhere claim attention;
But *I* have none of these on hand,—
For reasons I'll not mention.

ENVOY

So, come! though favors I bestow
Cannot be called extensive,
Who better than my friend should know
That they're at least expensive?

TO BARINE

If for your oath broken, or word lightly spoken,
A plague comes, Barine, to grieve you;
If on tooth or on finger a black mark shall linger
Your beauty to mar, I'll believe you.

But no sooner, the fact is, you bind, as your tact is,
Your head with the vows of untruth,
Than you shine out more charming, and, what's more alarming,
You come forth beloved of our youth.

It is advantageous, but no less outrageous,
Your poor mother's ashes to cheat;
While the gods of creation and each constellation
You seem to regard as your meat.

Now Venus, I own it, is pleased to condone it;
The good-natured nymphs merely smile;
And Cupid is merry,—'t is humorous, very,—
And sharpens his arrows the while.

Our boys you are making the slaves for your taking,
A new band is joined to the old;
While the horrified matrons your juvenile patrons
In vain would bring back to the fold.

The thrifty old fellows your loveliness mellows
Confess to a dread of your house;
But a more pressing duty, in view of your beauty,
Is the young wife's concern for her spouse.

THE RECONCILIATION

I

HE

When you were mine, in auld lang syne,
And when none else your charms might ogle,
I'll not deny, fair nymph, that I
Was happier than a heathen mogul.

SHE

Before *she* came, that rival flame
(Had ever mater saucier filia?),
In those good times, bepraised in rhymes,
I was more famed than Mother Ilia.

HE

Chloe of Thrace! With what a grace
Does she at song or harp employ her!
I'd gladly die, if only I
Could live forever to enjoy her!

SHE

My Sybaris so noble is
That, by the gods, I love him madly!
That I might save him from the grave,
I'd give my life, and give it gladly!

HE

What if *ma belle* from favor fell,
And I made up my mind to shake her;
Would Lydia then come back again,
And to her quondam love betake her?

SHE

My other beau should surely go,
And you alone should find me gracious;
For no one slings such odes and things

As does the lauriger Horatius!

THE RECONCILIATION

II

HORACE

While favored by thy smiles no other youth in amorous teasing
Around thy snowy neck his folding arms was wont to fling;
As long as I remained your love, acceptable and pleasing,
I lived a life of happiness beyond the Persian king.

LYDIA

While Lydia ranked Chloe in your unreserved opinion,
And for no other cherished thou a brighter, livelier flame,
I, Lydia, distinguished throughout the whole dominion,
Surpassed the Roman Ilia in eminence of fame.

HORACE

'T is now the Thracian Chloe whose accomplishments inthrall me,—
So sweet in modulations, such a mistress of the lyre.
In truth the fates, however terrible, could not appall me;
If they would spare her, sweet my soul, I gladly would expire.

LYDIA

And now the son of Ornytus, young Calais, inflames me
With mutual, restless passion and an all-consuming fire;
And if the fates, however dread, would spare the youth who claims me,
Not only once would I face death, but gladly twice expire.

HORACE

What if our early love returns to prove we were mistaken
And bind with brazen yoke the twain, to part, ah! nevermore?
What if the charming Chloe of the golden locks be shaken
And slighted Lydia again glide through the open door?

LYDIA

Though he is fairer than the star that shines so far above you,
Thou lighter than a cork, more stormy than the Adrian Sea,

Still should I long to live with you, to live for you and love you,
And cheerfully see death's approach if thou wert near to me.

THE ROASTING OF LYDIA

No more your needed rest at night
By ribald youth is troubled;
No more your windows, fastened tight,
Yield to their knocks redoubled.

No longer you may hear them cry,
"Why art thou, Lydia, lying
In heavy sleep till morn is nigh,
While I, your love, am dying?"

Grown old and faded, you bewail
The rake's insulting sally,
While round your home the Thracian gale
Storms through the lonely alley.

What furious thoughts will fill your breast,
What passions, fierce and tinglish
(Cannot be properly expressed
In calm, reposeful English).

Learn this, and hold your carping tongue:
Youth will be found rejoicing
In ivy green and myrtle young,
The praise of fresh life voicing;

And not content to dedicate,
With much protesting shiver,
The sapless leaves to winter's mate,
Hebrus, the cold dark river.

TO GLYCERA

The cruel mother of the Loves,

And other Powers offended,
Have stirred my heart, where newly roves
The passion that was ended.

'T is Glycera, to boldness prone,
Whose radiant beauty fires me;
While fairer than the Parian stone
Her dazzling face inspires me.

And on from Cyprus Venus speeds,
Forbidding—ah! the pity—
The Scythian lays, the Parthian meeds,
And such irrelevant ditty.

Here, boys, bring turf and vervain too;
Have bowls of wine adjacent;
And ere our sacrifice is through
She may be more complaisant.

TO LYDIA

I

When, Lydia, you (once fond and true,
But now grown cold and supercilious)
Praise Telly's charms of neck and arms—
Well, by the dog! it makes me bilious!

Then with despite my cheeks wax white,
My doddering brain gets weak and giddy,
My eyes o'erflow with tears which show
That passion melts my vitals, Liddy!

Deny, false jade, your escapade,
And, lo! your wounded shoulders show it!
No manly spark left such a mark—

Leastwise he surely was no poet!

With savage buss did Telephus
Abraid your lips, so plump and mellow;
As you would save what Venus gave,
I charge you shun that awkward fellow!

And now I say thrice happy they
That call on Hymen to requite 'em;
For, though love cools, the wedded fools
Must cleave till death doth disunite 'em.

TO LYDIA

II

When praising Telephus you sing
His rosy neck and waxen arms,
Forgetful of the pangs that wring
This heart for my neglected charms,

Soft down my cheek the tear-drop flows,
My color comes and goes the while,
And my rebellious liver glows,
And fiercely swells with laboring bile.

Perchance yon silly, passionate youth,
Distempered by the fumes of wine,
Has marred your shoulder with his tooth,
Or scarred those rosy lips of thine.

Be warned; he cannot faithful prove,
Who, with the cruel kiss you prize,
Has hurt the little mouth I love,
Where Venus's own nectar lies.

Whom golden links unbroken bind,
Thrice happy — more than thrice are they;

And constant, both in heart and mind,
In love await the final day.

TO QUINTIUS HIRPINUS

To Scythian and Cantabrian plots,
Pay them no heed, O Quintius!
So long as we
From care are free,
Vexations cannot cinch us.

Unwrinkled youth and grace, forsooth,
Speed hand in hand together;
The songs we sing
In time of spring
Are hushed in wintry weather.

Why, even flow'rs change with the hours,
And the moon has divers phases;
And shall the mind
Be racked to find
A clew to Fortune's mazes?

Nay; 'neath this tree let you and me
Woo Bacchus to caress us;
We're old, 't is true,
But still we two
Are thoroughbreds, God bless us!

While the wine gets cool in yonder pool,
Let's spruce up nice and tidy;
Who knows, old boy,
But we may decoy
The fair but furtive Lyde?

She can execute on her ivory lute
Sonatas full of passion,
And she bangs her hair

(Which is passing fair)
In the good old Spartan fashion.

WINE, WOMEN, AND SONG

Ovarus mine,
Plant thou the vine
Within this kindly soil of Tibur;
Nor temporal woes,
Nor spiritual, knows
The man who's a discreet imbiber.
For who doth croak
Of being broke,
Or who of warfare, after drinking?
With bowl atween us,
Of smiling Venus
And Bacchus shall we sing, I'm thinking.

Of symptoms fell
Which brawls impel,
Historic data give us warning;
The wretch who fights
When full, of nights,
Is bound to have a head next morning.
I do not scorn
A friendly horn,
But noisy toots, I can't abide 'em!
Your howling bat
Is stale and flat
To one who knows, because he's tried 'em!

The secrets of
The life I love
(Companionship with girls and toddy)
I would not drag
With drunken brag
Into the ken of everybody;
But in the shade

Let some coy maid
With smilax wreathe my flagon's nozzle,
Then all day long,
With mirth and song,
Shall I enjoy a quiet sozzle!

AN ODE TO FORTUNE

O Lady Fortune! 't is to thee I call,
Dwelling at Antium, thou hast power to crown
The veriest clod with riches and renown,
And change a triumph to a funeral
The tillers of the soil and they that vex the seas,
Confessing thee supreme, on bended knees
Invoke thee, all.

Of Dacian tribes, of roving Scythian bands,
Of cities, nations, lawless tyrants red
With guiltless blood, art thou the haunting dread;
Within thy path no human valor stands,
And, arbiter of empires, at thy frown
The sceptre, once supreme, slips surely down
From kingly hands.

Necessity precedes thee in thy way;
Hope fawns on thee, and Honor, too, is seen
Dancing attendance with obsequious mien;
But with what coward and abject dismay
The faithless crowd and treacherous wantons fly
When once their jars of luscious wine run dry,—
Such ingrates they!

Fortune, I call on thee to bless
Our king,—our Cæsar girt for foreign wars!
Help him to heal these fratricidal scars
That speak degenerate shame and wickedness;
And forge anew our impious spears and swords,
Wherewith we may against barbarian hordes

Our Past redress!

TO A JAR OF WINE

O gracious jar, — my friend, my twin,
Born at the time when I was born, —
Whether tomfoolery you inspire
Or animate with love's desire,
Or flame the soul with bitter scorn,
Or lull to sleep, O jar of mine!
Come from your place this festal day;
Corvinus hither wends his way,
And there's demand for wine!

Corvinus is the sort of man
Who dotes on tedious argument.
An advocate, his ponderous pate
Is full of Blackstone and of Kent;
Yet not insensible is he,
O genial Massic flood! to thee.
Why, even Cato used to take
A modest, surreptitious nip
At meal-times for his stomach's sake,
Or to forefend la grippe.

How dost thou melt the stoniest hearts,
And bare the cruel knave's design;
How through thy fascinating arts
We discount Hope, O gracious wine!
And passing rich the poor man feels
As through his veins thy affluence steals.

Now, prithee, make us frisk and sing,
And plot full many a naughty plot
With damsels fair — nor shall we care
Whether school keeps or not!
And whilst thy charms hold out to burn
We shall not deign to go to bed,
But we shall paint creation red;

So, fill, sweet wine, this friend of mine,—
My lawyer friend, as aforesaid.

TO POMPEIUS VARUS

Pompey, what fortune gives you back
To the friends and the gods who love you?
Once more you stand in your native land,
With your native sky above you.
Ah, side by side, in years agone,
We've faced tempestuous weather,
And often quaffed
The genial draught
From the same canteen together.

When honor at Philippi fell
A prey to brutal passion,
I regret to say that my feet ran away
In swift Iambic fashion.
You were no poet; soldier born,
You stayed, nor did you wince then.
Mercury came
To my help, which same
Has frequently saved me since then.

But now you're back, let's celebrate
In the good old way and classic;
Come, let us lard our skins with nard,
And bedew our souls with Massic!
With fillets of green parsley leaves
Our foreheads shall be done up;
And with song shall we
Protract our spree
Until the morrow's sun-up.

THE POET'S METAMORPHOSIS

Mæcenas, I propose to fly

To realms beyond these human portals;
No common things shall be my wings,
But such as sprout upon immortals.

Of lowly birth, once shed of earth,
Your Horace, precious (so you've told him),
Shall soar away; no tomb of clay
Nor Stygian prison-house shall hold him.

Upon my skin feathers begin
To warn the songster of his fleeting;
But never mind, I leave behind
Songs all the world shall keep repeating.

Lo! Boston girls, with corkscrew curls,
And husky westerns, wild and woolly,
And southern climes shall vaunt my rhymes,
And all profess to know me fully.

Methinks the West shall know me best,
And therefore hold my memory dearer;
For by that lake a bard shall make
My subtle, hidden meanings clearer.

So cherished, I shall never die;
Pray, therefore, spare your dolesome praises,
Your elegies, and plaintive cries,
For I shall fertilize no daisies!

TO VENUS

Venus, dear Cnidian-Paphian queen!
Desert that Cyprus way off yonder,
And fare you hence, where with incense
My Glycera would have you fonder;
And to your joy bring hence your boy,
The Graces with unbelted laughter,
The Nymphs, and Youth,—then, then, in sooth,

Should Mercury come tagging after.

IN THE SPRINGTIME

I

'T is spring! The boats bound to the sea;
The breezes, loitering kindly over
The fields, again bring herds and men
The grateful cheer of honeyed clover.

Now Venus hither leads her train;
The Nymphs and Graces join in orgies;
The moon is bright, and by her light
Old Vulcan kindles up his forges.

Bind myrtle now about your brow,
And weave fair flowers in maiden tresses;
Appease god Pan, who, kind to man,
Our fleeting life with affluence blesses;

But let the changing seasons mind us,
That Death's the certain doom of mortals,—
Grim Death, who waits at humble gates,
And likewise stalks through kingly portals.

Soon, Sestius, shall Plutonian shades
Enfold you with their hideous seemings;
Then love and mirth and joys of earth
Shall fade away like fevered dreamings.

IN THE SPRINGTIME

II

The western breeze is springing up, the ships are in the bay,
And spring has brought a happy change as winter melts away.
No more in stall or fire the herd or plowman finds delight;
No longer with the biting frosts the open fields are white.

Our Lady of Cythera now prepares to lead the dance,
While from above the kindly moon gives an approving glance;
The Nymphs and comely Graces join with Venus and the choir,
And Vulcan's glowing fancy lightly turns to thoughts of fire.

Now it is time with myrtle green to crown the shining pate,
And with the early blossoms of the spring to decorate;
To sacrifice to Faunus, on whose favor we rely,
A sprightly lamb, mayhap a kid, as he may specify.

Impartially the feet of Death at huts and castles strike;
The influenza carries off the rich and poor alike.
O Sestius, though blessed you are beyond the common run,
Life is too short to cherish e'en a distant hope begun.

The Shades and Pluto's mansion follow hard upon the grip.
Once there you cannot throw the dice, nor taste the wine you sip;
Nor look on blooming Lycidas, whose beauty you commend,
To whom the girls will presently their courtesies extend.

TO A BULLY

You, blatant coward that you are,
Upon the helpless vent your spite.
Suppose you ply your trade on me;
Come, monkey with this bard, and see
How I'll repay your bark with bite!

Ay, snarl just once at me, you brute!
And I shall hound you far and wide,
As fiercely as through drifted snow
The shepherd dog pursues what foe
Skulks on the Spartan mountain-side.

The chip is on my shoulder—see?
But touch it and I'll raise your fur;
I'm full of business, so beware!
For, though I'm loaded up for bear,
I'm quite as like to kill a cur!

TO MOTHER VENUS

O mother Venus, quit, I pray,
Your violent assailing!
The arts, forsooth, that fired my youth
At last are unavailing;
My blood runs cold, I'm getting old,
And all my powers are failing.

Speed thou upon thy white swans' wings,
And elsewhere deign to mellow
With thy soft arts the anguished hearts
Of swains that writhe and bellow;
And right away seek out, I pray,
Young Paullus,—he's your fellow!

You'll find young Paullus passing fair,
Modest, refined, and tony;
Go, now, incite the favored wight!
With Venus for a crony
He'll outshine all at feast and ball
And conversazione!

Then shall that godlike nose of thine
With perfumes be requited,
And then shall prance in Salian dance
The girls and boys delighted,
And while the lute blends with the flute
Shall tender loves be plighted.

But as for me, as you can see,
I'm getting old and spiteful.

I have no mind to female kind,
That once I deemed delightful;
No more brim up the festive cup
That sent me home at night full.

Why do I falter in my speech,
O cruel Ligurine?
Why do I chase from place to place
In weather wet and shiny?
Why down my nose forever flows
The tear that's cold and briny?

TO LYDIA

Tell me, Lydia, tell me why,
By the gods that dwell above,
Sybaris makes haste to die
Through your cruel, fatal love.

Now he hates the sunny plain;
Once he loved its dust and heat.
Now no more he leads the train
Of his peers on coursers fleet.

Now he dreads the Tiber's touch,
And avoids the wrestling-rings,—
He who formerly was such
An expert with quoits and things.

Come, now, Mistress Lydia, say
Why your Sybaris lies hid,
Why he shuns the martial play,
As we're told Achilles did.

TO NEOBULE

A sorry life, forsooth, these wretched girls are undergoing,
Restrained from draughts of pleasant wine, from loving favors

showing,
For fear an uncle's tongue a reprimand will be bestowing!

Sweet Cytherea's winged boy deprives you of your spinning,
And Hebrus, Neobule, his sad havoc is beginning,
Just as Minerva thriftily gets ready for an inning.

Who could resist this gallant youth, as Tiber's waves he breasted,
Or when the palm of riding from Bellerophon he wrested,
Or when with fists and feet the sluggers easily he bested?

He shot the fleeing stags with regularity surprising;
The way he intercepted boars was quite beyond surmising,—
No wonder that your thoughts this youth has been monopolizing!

So I repeat that with these maids fate is unkindly dealing,
Who never can in love's affair give license to their feeling,
Or share those sweet emotions when a gentle jag is stealing.

AT THE BALL GAME

What gods or heroes, whose brave deeds none can dispute,
Will you record, O Clio, on the harp and flute?
What lofty names shall sportive Echo grant a place
On Pindus' crown or Helicon's cool, shadowy space?

Sing not, my Orpheus, sweeping oft the tuneful strings,
Of gliding streams and nimble winds and such poor things;
But lend your measures to a theme of noble thought,
And crown with laurel these great heroes, as you ought.

Now steps Ryanus forth at call of furious Mars,
And from his oaken staff the sphere speeds to the stars;
And now he gains the tertiary goal, and turns,
While whiskered balls play round the timid staff of Burns.

Lo! from the tribunes on the bleachers comes a shout,
Beseeching bold Ansonius to line 'em out;
And as Apollo's flying chariot cleaves the sky,
So stanch Ansonius lifts the frightened ball on high.

Like roar of ocean beating on the Cretan cliff,

The strong Komiske gives the panting sphere a biff;
And from the tribunes rise loud murmurs everywhere,
When twice and thrice Mikellius beats the mocking air.

And as Achilles' fleet the Trojan waters sweeps,
So horror sways the throng, — Pfefferius sleeps!
And stalwart Konnor, though by Mercury inspired,
The Equus Carolus defies, and is retired.

So waxes fierce the strife between these godlike men;
And as the hero's fame grows by Virgilian pen,
So let Clarksonius Maximus be raised to heights
As far above the moon as moon o'er lesser lights.

But as for me, the ivy leaf is my reward,
If you a place among the lyric bards accord;
With crest exalted, and O "People," with delight,
I'll proudly strike the stars, and so be out of sight.

EPILOGUE

The day is done; and, lo! the shades
Melt 'neath Diana's mellow grace.
Hark, how those deep, designing maids
Feign terror in this sylvan place!
Come, friends, it's time that we should go;
We're honest married folk, you know.

Was not the wine delicious cool
Whose sweetness Pyrrha's smile enhanced?
And by that clear Bandusian pool
How gayly Chloe sung and danced!
And Lydia Die, — aha, methinks
You'll not forget the saucy minx!

But, oh, the echoes of those songs
That soothed our cares and lulled our hearts!
Not to that age nor this belongs
The glory of what heaven-born arts
Speak with the old distinctive charm

From yonder humble Sabine farm!

The day is done. Now off to bed,
Lest by some rural ruse surprised,
And by those artful girls misled,
You two be sadly compromised.
You go; perhaps *I*'d better stay
To shoo the giddy things away!

But sometime we shall meet again
Beside Digentia, cool and clear,—
You and we twain, old friend; and then
We'll have our fill of pagan cheer.
Then, could old Horace join us three,
How proud and happy he would be!

Or if we part to meet no more
This side the misty Stygian Sea,
Be sure of this: on yonder shore
Sweet cheer awaiteth such as we;
A Sabine pagan's heaven, O friend,—
The fellowship that knows no end!

E.F.